Up and Away

D0812994

For my dear son, Ed.
I made him ride his bike
without stabilisers!

Find out more about **Ricky Rocket** at
www.shoo-rayner.co.uk

ORCHARD BOOKS
338 Euston Road, London NW1 3BH
Orchard Books Australia
Hachette Children's Books
Level 17/207 Kent St, Sydney, NSW 2000

ISBN 1 84616 038 3 (hardback)
ISBN 1 84616 393 5 (paperback)

First published in 2006 by Orchard Books
First paperback publication in 2007

Text and illustrations © Shoo Rayner 2006

1 3 5 7 9 10 8 6 4 2 (hardback)
1 3 5 7 9 10 8 6 4 2 (paperback)

Printed in Great Britain
Orchard Books is a division of Hachette Children's Books

Up and Away

Shoo Rayner

ORCHARD BOOKS

"BUM!" Ricky yelled.

"MUuum! Ricky's swearing,"
screamed Ricky's little sister, Sue.

"I'm not swearing," said Ricky.

"Yes you are!" Sue was the most irritating little girl in the universe.

Ricky raised his voice. "B. U. M. stands for *Brilliantly Utterly Magnificent*, actually!"

Mum folded her arms. "And *what* is so Brilliantly Utterly Magnificent?"

"This is!" Ricky held up the free gift from his Vorg Flakes. "They're stickers for your rocket," he explained. "They make it look like you've been in a laser fight with the evil Lord Vorg."

"BUM!" said Dad.

"Don't you start!" said Mum, rolling her eyes.

Dad bit off a huge mouthful of toast. "Mmf abltm uu neerned awie avout pabiltherz!"

Sue pointed at Dad. "It's rude to speak with your mouth full."

"Sue's right," said Mum. "How is Ricky ever going to learn any manners?"

But Ricky understood what Dad had said. He shivered. This was going to be a big day for him.

Dad swallowed his toast. "I said, it's time Ricky learned to fly without stabilisers."

"Oh BUM!" whooped Ricky.

FLYING WITHOUT STABILISERS

Rogon Squid can fly before they can walk. All other creatures learn by using **stabilisers**.

Ricky's rocket came with UPRITE® Gravity Balls bolted on the outside.

Gravity Balls control the rocket, allowing it to go either **up** or **sideways.**

Stabilised rockets can only be flown with junior control equipment.

"**Hey, Dad! They've got** the new Nano-micro drives and look...over there...Star Seeker ⓈⓇ navigation pads." Ricky followed Dad down the aisles of the Galactic Rocket Store.

"Here we are!" said Dad, in the junior section.

"Whoah!" Ricky's eyes nearly popped out of his head. "A Lord Vorg Helmet," he cooed.

Dad tut-tutted. "That's a toy. You need a proper helmet. Got a GFB3000?" he asked the salesman.

The salesman brought them a large transparent bowl and put it over Ricky's head.

"But it looks like a goldfish bowl!" Ricky complained.

"That's what G.F.B. stands for!" the salesman laughed. "The Gold Fish Bowl 3000! Not the latest fashion, but still the best helmet in the universe."

Dad smiled. "We'll need
a new control handle too."

"Ah!" the salesman nodded.
"Is someone learning to fly
without stabilisers?"

"Me!" Ricky said. "Dad's
teaching me this afternoon."

"You'll want the Fly-rite XG." The salesman pressed something into Ricky's hand. "Try this."

"It sort of shapes itself to my hand," Ricky said, surprised. "It feels as though I've used it all my life."

The salesman winked. "Good luck!"

THE GALACTIC ROCKET STORE

Also known as **"the BIG G"** and also **GRS**.

There's a store on the edge of **every** town in the Galaxy. There is **always** ample parking and docking.

It's the only place to get the **GFB 3000**. They may be out of date, but **retro** is back in fashion!

You can always get fresh **Murgle maggots** in the **Big G**. They're the best bait for **deep space fishing**.

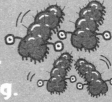

The stabilisers had been on Ricky's rocket as long as he could remember. The bolts were rusty.

"Blast!" The spanner slipped. Dad had hurt his little finger.

"MUuum! Daddy's swearing!" Sue screamed.

"Blast is not a swear word!" Dad yelled. "B.L.A.S.T stands for *Blooming Lousy Awful Stupid Thing*!"

Mum steered Sue into the house. "Let's leave them alone. We'll come back when your father has calmed down!"

The last bolt was so rusty, Dad had
to cut through it with a laserblade.

"It looks really different
without stabilisers," Ricky said.

"It's...well...like a real rocket!

Dad fitted the Fly-rite XG and showed Ricky how to use it. "Just remember these four letters: C.L.I.P."

"C.L.I.P." Ricky whispered, as he put his new helmet on. "What does it stand for, Dad?"

Dad slapped Ricky on the back. "*Crash Landing Is Painful*!"

Dad's voice filled Ricky's helmet speakers. "Just keep your balance and off you go!"

"Power up!" Ricky spoke into his microphone. The rocket lifted and inched forward.

Dad's voice crackled loudly in his
ears. "It's rolling to the left!"

Ricky pulled hard on the control stick.
"Now it's rolling to the right!"

Ricky panicked. "The stabilisers never let me lean over so far!"

"Now you're spinning!"

Ricky waggled the controls. The rocket wobbled and spun.

"USE YOUR BRAKES!" Dad's scream filled Ricky's helmet.

Ricky felt as though his brain was being scrambled like eggs. He felt the rocket tumble head over heels. He was going to crash. Where were the brakes?

There were stars in front of Ricky's eyes. "I'm flying through space!" he muttered dreamily.

"No you're not," Dad's voice hissed in his ear. "You're lying in Mr Dargon's vegetables!"

Mr Dargon's angry face appeared in Ricky's window. He was turning three shades of purple and shaking his tentacles.

MR DARGON'S
SPACE VEGETABLES

Mr Dargon, or **Spud** to his friends, is **half vegetable** himself. He can't make food from sunlight, but he does need **watering** once a day.

Mr Dargon is the Warden of his garden, which is a **retirement home** for ancient vegetables.

Mrs Sprout is one hundred and eighty three.

Mr Zucchini is **ninety-two** and he can remember when vegetables were **cooked** and **eaten**.

Nowadays **organic** food is made in hyper-clean factories.

Ricky worked hard all afternoon, but the rocket kept crashing and falling over.

Every time Ricky felt he was getting the hang of it, Dad shouted orders at him, making him panic and lose control.

"OK. Just one more time," Dad ordered.

Ricky snapped into the microphone. "No!"
"What do you mean, 'No'?" Dad shouted.

33

Ricky pressed a small green button on the front of his helmet. Dad's voice cut out and Ricky relaxed. He could see Dad waving his arms in the air and shouting...but he couldn't hear him.

Ricky took the controls and spoke to the rocket. "OK, let's fly."

FIVE IRRITATING THINGS ABOUT DADS

They **always think they** know best!

They think you will **understand** if they **shout** loud enough!

They have to drill holes in things!

They won't let you have the **teevee** remote control!

They're always **kissing** and **cuddling** mums!

Without Dad "helping", Ricky found flying the most natural thing in the world.

"Engines on!" Ricky instructed the craft.

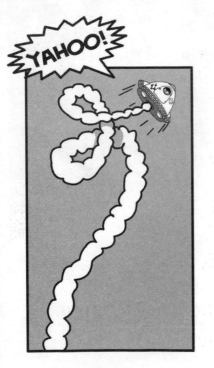

"Ease the brake off." This time, Ricky felt the Fly-rite XG respond to every tiny movement he made.

"I've got you!" Ricky told the little craft. He was in complete control. With each circuit he felt more confident.

Ricky pressed the green sound button and the helmet filled with Dad's happy whooping.

"Well done, son!" he was shouting. "Now pull back, slowly!"

Ricky had seen Lord Vorg do it
a million times on the teevee. Ricky
imagined a fleet of spaceships waiting
to do battle in orbit. Only he could save
the planet now!

Gently, he squeezed back the throttle.

The seat throbbed. The engine roared
and the rocket hurtled into the sky.

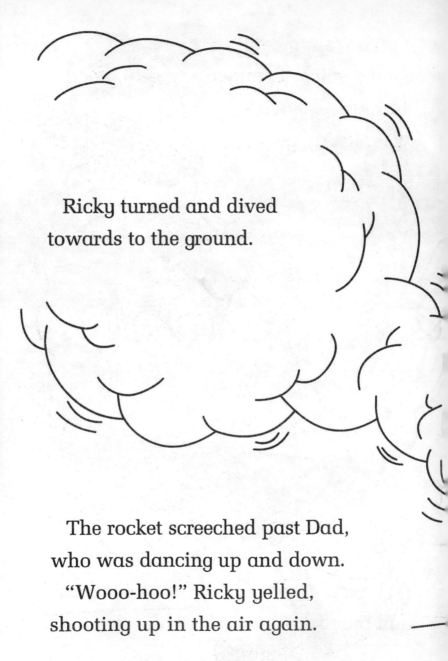

Ricky turned and dived
towards to the ground.

The rocket screeched past Dad,
who was dancing up and down.
"Wooo-hoo!" Ricky yelled,
shooting up in the air again.

"That's my boy!"
Dad's voice screamed
from the speakers.
"Go, Ricky, go!"

Ricky swooped and
whooshed, climbed
and dived. In his
head he was Lord Vorg,
Master of the Universe,
the greatest fighter pilot
there has ever been.

"Entering
vertical descent
stage," Ricky
spoke the words
he heard every
week on the Lord
Vorg teevee show.
    He landed
perfectly, right
in front of the
kitchen door.

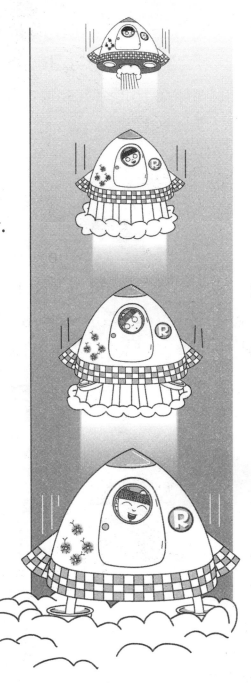

Sue was waiting for him.

"You're not allowed to land so close to the house," she nagged in her horrid, sing-song, know-it-all voice. "It's really dangerous!"

Ricky ignored her. He was a proper pilot now. Flying without stabilisers was almost like being grown-up.

"Did you see me?" he asked breathlessly.

Dad hugged him. "You were fantastic!" he said. "I think you were born to fly!"

45

Ricky looked at Mum's excited face. "Did you see me, Mum? What did you think?"

Mum laughed. "You were...BUTT!"

Dad and Ricky exchanged a look. Mum always got things wrong.

"You mean BUM!" they chorused.

"No," laughed Mum. "I mean
B.U.T.T. – *Brilliantly Utterly
Totally Terrific!*"

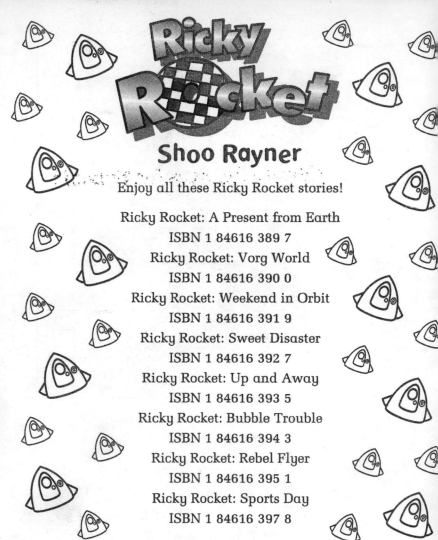

Ricky Rocket

Shoo Rayner

Enjoy all these Ricky Rocket stories!

All priced at £3.99

Orchard Crunchies are available from all good bookshops, or can be ordered
direct from the publisher: Orchard Books, PO BOX 29, Douglas IM99 1BQ
Credit card orders please telephone 01624 836000 or fax 01624 837033
or visit our internet site: www.wattspub.co.uk or e-mail: bookshop@enterprise.net for details.

To order please quote title, author and ISBN and your full name and address.
Cheques and postal orders should be made payable to 'Bookpost plc.'
Postage and packing is FREE within the UK
(overseas customers should add £1.00 per book).

Prices and availability are subject to change.